Dear Gos,
May you always
be surrounded by good
friends.
Merry Christmas 2005!
Love,
Aunt Kim,
Uncle Jesse,
+ Sydney

Louis & the Dodo

For Esther, a dear friend who happens to be my mom — MS

For Vi Vi and Nhi Nhi — VN

Special thanks to Meredith Mundy Wasinger, Frances Gilbert, and Katherine Nix.
You all made this book possible.

Library of Congress Cataloging-in-Publication Data Available

10 9 8 7 6 5 4 3 2 1

Published by Sterling Publishing Co., Inc.
387 Park Avenue South, New York, NY 10016
Text © 2005 by Mark Shulman
Illustrations © 2005 by Vincent Nguyen
Designed by Joe Bartos

Created at Oomf, Inc.
www.Oomf.com

Distributed in Canada by Sterling Publishing
C/o Canadian Manda Group, 165 Dufferin Street
Toronto, Ontario, Canada M6K 3H6
Distributed in Great Britain and Europe by Chris Lloyd at Orca Book
Services, Stanley House, Fleets Lane, Poole BH15 3AJ, England

Printed in China
All rights reserved

Sterling ISBN 1-4027-2872-7

For information about custom editions, special sales, premium and
corporate purchases, please contact Sterling Special Sales
Department at 800-805-5489 or specialsales@sterlingpub.com.

Louis & the Dodo

By Mark Shulman

Illustrated by Vincent Nguyen

Sterling Publishing Co., Inc.

New York

Louis couldn't even look at the baseball mitt his mother handed him.

"Those kids don't *want* to play with me," he whispered. "I'm not *like* them."

Louis didn't have people friends, and his parents worried.
But Louis knew all about friendship.

It meant helping…

and protecting…

and being brave.

And whenever Louis needed a friend,

someone was there for him, too.

As it so happens, the birds needed Louis that day more than ever. They twittered and circled above him. They showed him a poster they had found.

"Oh, my," said Louis. "Something has to be done."

Louis wasn't old enough to read, but the pictures said everything.
A sad little dodo bird was being kept in a circus. Clowns were making it do
dangerous tricks. Louis was scared for the Dodo. "I'll help that little bird
get home," promised Louis. "Wherever that is."

Like small red balloons, the cardinals carried Louis to the faraway circus grounds.

A circus is usually a thrilling place, but this one felt dark and cold and strange.

As strange as it looked on the outside, the tent was even stranger inside.

Performers scurried about, setting up their show. There were clowns high on stilts, clowns eating fire, and clowns doing flips. Some clowns were even dressed as birds. They treated Louis like one of their own.

"Come on, come on!" said a laughing clown, leading Louis toward
the giant cannon. "We can send you up just like the dodo!"
"You'll be safe and sound!" said the long-legged clown, high above Louis.
"And oh, what a sound! You're going to *fly*!"

Louis wriggled and slipped from their big gloves just in time.
He jumped behind colorful cloaks and dodged between giant legs.
"Where did he go?" yelled the moonfaced clown. Beyond the noise, and
past the confusion, Louis found himself at an old, dark cage.

Louis felt his heart pounding. He peered through the bars.

The dodo lay small in a corner, resting on straw, looking wearily at the boy.

Then Louis revealed the golden key the birds had given him.

Now the dodo sat forward. He recognized that special key.

This one, this person, had come as a friend.

It was easy for Louis to unlock the cage door, but leaving the tent would be much harder.

The clowns were coming closer. Louis stepped between the dodo and the clowns. He knew exactly what to do.

"Squawk! Squawk! Squawk!" cried Louis. "Squawk! Squawk! Squawk!" answered his friends, hiding in the highest shadows of the circus tent. Birds soared down from every direction to help save Louis and the dodo.

The clowns ran every which way to escape the swooping flock. The colorful birds dived and flapped, toppling the tall ones and tickling the tiny ones. Clowns fell upon clowns in a great, ridiculous heap.

Quickly and quietly, the two new friends escaped the circus tent.
No one saw them leave.

In the calm night air, they slipped into the basket of the balloon ride.
While Louis watched the tent, the dodo cut each rope with quick, clean bites.
The great balloon climbed up and beyond the trees.

Over the gentle clouds and under the smiling moon they soared together, following the winds toward home.

Home was a hidden island paradise for birds of every size and color.
There were warm breezes and rolling green hills spreading out to the sea.
Melodies of birdsong filled the air. Louis felt a joy that had no words.

The dodo's family was thrilled to have their little one back.
Louis shared their happiness, but he stood apart. "I don't want to
be in the way," he said to himself. "Maybe I don't belong here, either."

The little dodo told all the birds how brave Louis had been.
The grateful flock made a friendship circle around the boy.
They nuzzled his arms and sang their secret songs to him.
Before long, the rising sun turned the dawn into morning.

"It's daytime," said Louis, feeling ready to cry. "I want to stay.
But it's time to go home. My parents will wake up and worry."
His eyes filled with tears as he looked slowly across the island and out
to sea. Once he found home, could he ever return to his new friends?

By way of an answer, the oldest dodo guided Louis to a
small hill. Set inside the grassy slope was a wooden door
with a golden keyhole. This, he thought, is how you return.

Louis brought out his special key and scraped it against the old lock.
The rusty hinges moaned.

"It's my closet!" cried Louis. "There's a door in my closet!
I can come back!" Louis chirped and jumped with pleasure,
hugging his little dodo friend.

"And you can come visit me in my room!"

The birds shook their heads. Only a child could pass through
the hillside door. But Louis could venture back any time he wished.

And every night after his parents went to sleep, that's exactly what he did.

THE END